P9-ARL-763

THE POOL PARTY

OTHER YEARLING BOOKS YOU WILL ENJOY:

YEARLING BOOKS are designed especially to entertain and enlighten young people. Patricia Reilly Giff, consultant to this series, received her bachelor's degree from Marymount College and a master's degree in history from St. John's University. She holds a Professional Diploma in Reading and a Doctorate of Humane Letters from Hofstra University. She was a teacher and reading consultant for many years, and is the author of numerous books for young readers.

For a complete listing of all Yearling titles, write to
Dell Readers Service,
P.O. Box 1045,
South Holland, IL 60473.

GARY SOTO

The
Pool Party

Illustrated by Robert Casilla

A YEARLING BOOK

Published by
Bantam Doubleday Dell Books for Young Readers
a division of
Bantam Doubleday Dell Publishing Group, Inc.
1540 Broadway
New York, New York 10036

ISBN: 0-440-41010-X

Reprinted by arrangement with Delacorte Press
Printed in the United States of America

July 1995

10 9 8 7 6 5 4 3 2 1

CWO

THE POOL PARTY

You are invited to
Tiffany Perez's
~ Pool Party ~
Saturday from 12 noon – 4 pm
1334 The Bluff

Chapter 1

It was Saturday, summer vacation, but a workday for the Herrera family. The sun, a yellow bonnet of summer heat, hung above the trees. Rudy's entire family—father, mother, sister, and grandfather, who was known throughout Fresno as "El Shorty"— were working in the yard. Father was a gardener, but his yard was brimming with tall, scraggly weeds.

Rudy was in the kitchen slapping

together a sandwich for his older sister, Estela. He owed her a favor. She had promised to do more yard work if he sneaked into the house to make a sandwich.

"Make it thick," Estela had told Rudy. "Three slices of bologna and some cheese."

Rudy layered the sandwich with only one slice of bologna, tomato, and potato chips. When he pressed his palm against the sandwich, the chips crunched. He liked that sound, and liked how the sliced tomato would bleed a faint pinkish juice. He peeked into the sandwich. The bologna looked like a tongue wagging at him.

He picked up the sandwich and looked out the kitchen window. His mother, hair tied with a bandanna, was vacuuming the trunk of their battered Oldsmobile. Rudy imagined the vacuum sucking up marbles, bottle caps, candy wrappers, and leaves. He saw one of his gym socks gag the hose. Mother made a face and wrestled with the sock.

When his mother turned around, Rudy

ducked down, his back to the wall. His heart pounded, not from fear but from the giddiness of sneaking around behind his mother's back.

As Rudy stood up, he saw a letter on the kitchen table. The letter was addressed to him. He put the sandwich down and licked his salty fingers before opening up the letter. When he tore it open, glitter rained onto the kitchen table. It was like magic, or a rainbow that had collapsed in his own house. He read

You are invited to Tiffany Perez's
Pool Party
Saturday, from 12 noon–4 P.M.
1334 The Bluffs

"What's a 'pool party'?" he wondered aloud. He sniffed the envelope, nostrils quivering. It smelled like the stuff his mother would dab on her wrists on those evenings she went dancing with his father.

Rudy ran out the back door with the sandwich and the invitation, which trailed a sweet scent of perfume. His grandfather, El Shorty, was sitting in the yard, taping a splintered shovel.

"*Abuelo, mira!*" Rudy shouted, waving the invitation. The sandwich flopped in his hand, a slice of tomato falling out.

Not even thinking about it, Grandfather took the sandwich from Rudy and chomped a big corner from it. He chewed and cleared his throat. "*Mira,* it's good as new," he said of the shovel. "I had this shovel fourteen years. It dug up and buried a lot of things, *mi'jo.*"

Grandfather took another bite of the sandwich and began a long story about how once when he was a young man hitchhiking to California his shoes were stolen and he had to use cardboard to jump from place to place.

"Like this," Grandfather explained. He demonstrated how he would pitch the cardboard in front of him, step on it, let his feet cool for a few seconds before he would step off the cardboard and pitch it again in front of him. That's how he jumped from place to place and ended up in Fresno, working as a gardener. That's how years later he would be sitting in the backyard taping a splintered shovel back to life.

Rudy was familiar with this story. He had heard it a hundred times, maybe more, and other stories about the usefulness of electrical tape, another topic that made Rudy wonder if his grandfather was all right in the head. His grandfather was always telling stories about the poor days in California, just after he arrived from Mexico with the dream of a home and an orange tree in the backyard.

Rudy stopped his grandfather's monologue by shoving the invitation in his face. "Grandpa, what's a pool party?" he asked.

His grandfather studied the invitation, and then, scratching his stubbled face, said, "That's when a bunch of guys get together and shoot pool. Like me and my *compa* Pete Salinas when we—"

"Shoot pool?" Rudy interrupted. It didn't seem right. Tiffany was the richest girl at his school. Rudy couldn't picture her leaning over a pool table, muttering, "Eight ball in the side pocket."

"Yeah, like when me and Pete Salinas," his grandfather started, "were down to our last quarter and we found ourselves without shirts—"

Rudy rolled his eyes, because the story sounded familiar. Pretending to be startled, Rudy shouted, "It's the phone," and ran away. He ran to the side of the house where his mother was vacuuming the car. "Mom!" he screamed over the wail of the vacuum. "Mom, I got invited to Tiffany's pool party! What's a 'pool party'?"

His mother turned and, by accident, the invitation was sucked into the hose, which gagged and moaned before the card descended into the belly of the vacuum.

"The invitation!" Rudy screamed. He hastily turned off the vacuum and opened it up. He plucked out the invitation, which was crinkled but still sweet-smelling. He also plucked out and pocketed a marble he had been looking for.

"Look," Rudy said, flapping the invitation at his mother.

Mother took the invitation and read it slowly. She smelled it, a wrinkle cutting across her brow. "*¿Quién es* Tiffany Perez?"

"A girl at school."

"A girl?" Rudy's mother looked curiously at him. She smelled the invitation a second time and handed it back.

"*No sé*. I don't know what a 'pool party' is," Mother finally said. "Ask Estela."

Rudy trotted away, his untied laces slapping around his ankles, and passed his father, who was carrying a plastic trash bag over his shoulders. "Hey, Dad! I'm invited to a pool party," Rudy boasted.

"That's good," Father said. "Give me five, *hombre*. No, ten! No, fifteen and twenty."

They slapped palms and spun away. But Rudy's father stopped in his tracks. He

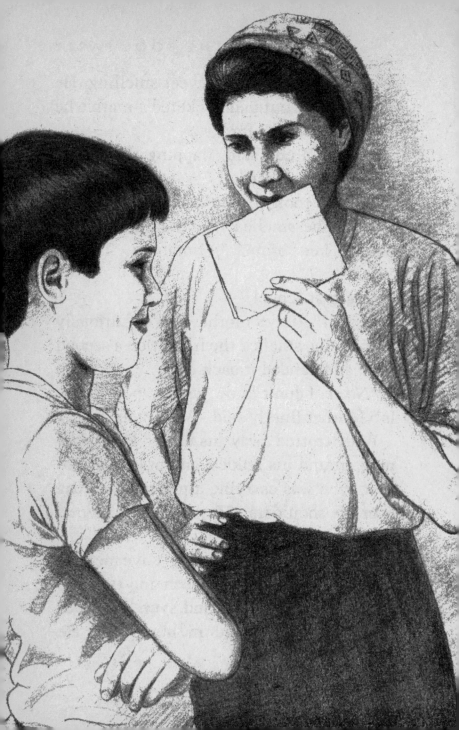

looked back at his son, his head tilted in wonder. "What's a 'pool party'?" he asked. He shrugged and lifted the trash bag onto his shoulders.

Rudy approached his sister, Estela, who was raking grass clippings. Her hair was tangled, and she looked hot. A mustache of sweat clung to her upper lip.

"Where have you been?" Estela snapped. "Where's my sandwich?"

"Grandpa ate it."

"Grandpa ate it!" she screamed. Her eyebrows became arched with anger. "Forget it. Don't expect me to do extra work now. Rudy, you're such a—"

"Look, Estela," Rudy said. He shoved the invitation at his sister. She unfolded the invitation and read it. She looked at her brother and asked, "Tiffany Perez invited you to her house? Isn't she real rich?"

"I guess," Rudy said, shrugging his shoulders. He figured that anyone who had more than a dollar fifty was rich. He had a pinch of dimes and nickels, and a few pennies tucked away in his drawer. At last count he had almost two dollars to his name.

She sniffed the invitation. "Why would Tiffany want you there?"

Rudy thought about that for a second and answered, "Maybe she likes my style."

"Get real," Estela growled, then added with kindness, "Rudy, a 'pool party' is a swim party. You have to be polite. You can't eat with your fingers."

"Oh, it's that kind of party," Rudy said, a light coming on inside his head. He pictured himself wiping his mouth every time he took a bite of food or sipped a drink.

Just then Rudy's best friend rode up on his bike.

"What's happening?" asked Alex.

"Look at this, Alex," Rudy said, shoving his invitation at his friend.

Alex read the invitation three times, his lips moving over each word. He licked his lips. "*Híjole*, Tiffany Perez is rich. You're going to eat good."

Chapter 2

"We got a job. Let's go! *Ándale!*" Rudy's father called from the back steps. Rudy and his grandfather were in the yard playing cards. They wore baseball caps that shaded their eyes like gamblers.

Rudy's father was a gardener in spring and summer and a house painter in fall and winter. Now that they were deep into July, his knees were stained green, and his hands resembled roots dug up from the earth. He worked for widows and retired people, and a few rich families whose driveways were long and smooth as glass.

Today, it was a rich person's house in North Fresno. Rudy, his father, and grandfather, all dressed in khaki, were climbing into their Oldsmobile. The mowers, rakes, and broom stuck out from the trunk.

Just as they were ready to leave, Rudy's mother came out of the house with a Polaroid camera dangling from her wrist.

"*Espérate,*" she yelled, and waved.

"Look, Mom's gonna take a picture," Rudy said. A big, *queso* smile cut across his face.

Grandfather smoothed his work shirt and played with his collar. He combed his hair with his stubby fingers.

"Let me take a picture," she said. She looked into the viewer. "Rudy, you're smiling too big."

Rudy relaxed his smile.

The three of them stood, arm in arm, with Rudy in the middle. They smiled like pumpkins when Rudy's mother, one eye squinted, sang, "*Queso.*" The camera shuddered and clicked, and a picture the size of a slice of cheese rolled noisily out of the camera.

Rudy's mother tore off the picture. She was known for her shaky hand. Sometimes their heads were cut off, and other times they were completely out of the frame and only their lean shadows on the ground would be seen. Still, she would proudly prop them up on the television or tape them to the refrigerator, a family of blurred faces.

Rudy's father tapped his work boot as they waited for their faces to develop out of the fog of Polaroid land.

Today, only the tops of their heads were cut off.

"Baby," Rudy's father said, "you almost got it right."

"Yeah, Mom, you did a good job," Rudy said in encouragement.

They piled into the car and drove across town, their equipment rattling in the trunk. The small houses gave way to large houses, all set way back from the street.

"You see, *mi'jo*," Rudy's grandfather said. "This is how to live."

"Yeah, I wouldn't mind having a little *casita* like one of these," Father said. A toothpick dangled from the corner of his mouth.

They admired the houses and the calm lushness of shrubs and bushes deep with shadows. The sprinklers were hissing on the lawns and pampered dogs with tags jingling a tinny music on their collars paced up and down the walk.

Father stopped at a large house, and all of them got out and stretched.

"*Híjole, es muy grande!*" Grandfather whistled.

"Like Club Med," Rudy's father remarked as he untied the trunk and took out a bundle of rakes and shovels. "Come on, let's go."

A woman appeared on the front steps. "Yoo-hoo," she called, waving a delicate finger that sparkled with a blue diamond. "Mr. Herrera, perfect timing. My children are at ballet."

"Hello, Mrs. Gentry," Father greeted her. "Want us to cut the front first?"

"That's a perfect idea." Mrs. Gentry scanned her yard and inhaled the morning air. "Isn't it just lovely?"

"What?" Rudy asked, looking around. "What's lovely?"

"The morning," she said. She smiled and walked away with her nose lifted and sniffing the air.

The three of them looked at each other, and shrugged their shoulders.

"*Qué loca*," Grandfather said as he returned to the car for his hat and work gloves.

They started the mowers, the engines coughing blue smoke. While his grandfather and father cut and edged the lawns, Rudy gathered the clippings. He raked most of them into a burlap sack, and then swept up the blades of grass from the walk. With

shears he snipped the grass around the sprinkler heads. He felt like a barber and giggled when he remembered how a friend had cut his hair and left him as bald as the belly of a green-spotted frog.

While they were working on their hands and knees, Father found a nickel minted in 1949.

"Hey, Little Rudy, check this out," he yelled.

Rudy was standing on a small ladder, pruning flowering quince. He jumped down and, with his grandfather in tow, ran over to see what his father was yelling about.

"*Mira, hijo,*" Father said. He handed Rudy the dirt-caked nickel. "It's worth *mucho dinero.* See that 'D'?"

"Yeah," Rudy said, examining it closely.

"That means it was minted in Denver, Colorado," Father explained.

Rudy took the coin in his hands. To him, 1949 seemed like the beginning of the world—long, long ago, just about the time the dinosaurs died out.

"Wow," Rudy sighed as he turned it over admiringly. "Can I have it—please?" Rudy gave his father a pleading puppy-dog look.

"I'll flip you for it," Father said.

"Fair deal."

Father flipped the nickel into the air, almost tree level, and when it came down and smacked against his father's wrist, Rudy called, "Heads." Father peeked with a squinting eye. It was tails. But Father turned his wrist and whined, "Ah, man, it was heads. You win, Rudy."

"All right!" Rudy yelled. He pocketed the coin, and even listened with patience to his grandfather's story of how he was once down to a nickel, two oranges, and a sweater with worn elbows. This was way before 1949, in the time of dinosaurs.

They returned to work. They cut the backyard lawn, the air scented with the smell of cut grass. They worked continuously, stopping only to drink from the garden hose.

In the backyard, the Gentry's kidney-shaped pool gleamed a blue tint. Rudy stood at the pool's edge, looking down where sunlight danced on the water. He knew from experience that his face was sweaty from work, and that a necklace of dirt darkened his throat. He remembered Tiffany Perez's pool party the coming Saturday. Rudy wondered if her yard was as large as this one. Even in the far corner, near a fig tree, a white doghouse stood tall as a wedding cake.

Grandfather tiptoed up from behind. He grabbed Rudy's shoulders and pretended to shove him into the water.

"No!" Rudy screamed.

"You look hot, *chamaco*," Grandfather laughed. He held Rudy over the water. Rudy kicked his legs and begged not to be thrown in.

"Knock it off, we're almost done," Father

yelled. He was holding up a pair of shiny pruning shears. "Let's do the bush."

Finally, when they finished and had piled the equipment back into the trunk, Mrs. Gentry came out to inspect the work. She was happy. Her smile made folds in her face.

"Now, let's see, Mr. Herrera," she said. "We agreed on forty-five dollars."

"That's right, ma'am," he said.

"I thought it was fifty-five," Grandfather said in Spanish. "Did she charge us for drinking from her hose?"

"No, *hombre*, forty-five," Father said in Spanish. "I got it right."

The three stood in a line. Mrs. Gentry counted out dollar bills. "One, two, three..." When she counted out fifteen, Grandfather snatched a bill from Father's palm. Mrs. Gentry shot a curious look at Grandfather, then continued counting out the dollar bills. When she got to twenty, Grandfather snatched another dollar bill. She looked at him even more curiously.

Rudy's father whispered in Spanish, "What're you doing?"

"I don't know," Grandfather said. "I can't help myself. The money looks so tempting."

"Knock it off, *hombre*," Father growled. He smiled at Mrs. Gentry and said, "Grandpa's been in the sun too long."

Grandfather shrugged his shoulders and winked at his grandson, who winked back and fumbled for the nickel in his pocket.

Mrs. Gentry counted out the remaining amount, and when she finished, she opened her purse and brought out a tiny striped candy cane.

"And this is for you, my little man," she said, handing it to Rudy.

Rudy took the candy cane and said, "Thank you."

Mrs. Gentry smiled and thanked him with a poorly pronounced, *"De nada. Gracias a ustedes."* She lifted her nose and sniffed the air. "It's a lovely morning."

The three looked at each other. They were certain that she was *loca*.

When they got to the car, Rudy unwrapped the candy cane and placed it inside his bottom lip like a fish hook. While they rattled away in their car, Rudy sucked the stripes from the candy cane.

Chapter 3

Rudy and his best friend, Alex, stood at the stove making peanut butter tortillas, a midmorning treat. Estela sat at the table, painting her fingernails. She had a new boyfriend, a boy named Lucky, and she was waiting for his phone call. He was in bed with a hurt knee. He had fallen from his skateboard and snapped a bone whose name sounded something like *papas* or *papi* or Pepsi. Rudy thought Lucky wasn't very lucky. Later, Rudy learned from his mother that it was his patela, the knee-cap.

"Rudy," his sister said, not looking up as she stroked red enamel on her fingernails, "you better take something to Tiffany's party."

"I am. I'm taking a towel," he said. He snatched his tortilla from the burner. The flames were like the petals of a blue flower, but hot.

"No, I mean more than that."

"Mom says I can take only one towel."

"No, *menso*, take something to share," Estela snickered at her brother. She wondered how he could have gotten through his first ten years of life without a lesson in manners. "Rudy, I know some of Tiffany's friends. I don't want you to make a fool of yourself—or embarrass me!" She knew that Tiffany's party would be a hit.

"Don't worry. I'll be cool," Rudy said. "I'll show them some belly flops."

"Rudy, it's a pool party," Estela said. "You can't get your hair wet or monkey around in the water."

"We can't swim?" Rudy asked. "How come? It says on the invitation."

"Forget what it says," she said as she turned and faced her brother. "You see, you're just supposed to hang around the pool."

"But that's not fair. I like to swim."

"But you're not supposed to. You're just supposed to talk, have conversation." She made a face at her brother. "Look, Rudy, I'm trying to teach you manners."

"But I wanna fool around and have fun. Wouldn't you wanna swim, Alex?"

"Yeah, it's more fun," Alex agreed. "Anyway, Rudy already has manners." Alex licked the spoon and handed it to Rudy.

"You're not catching on," Estela whined. "It's no use, you're hopeless." She wanted to pull her hair and scream, and would have except her fingernails were wet.

"When is the pool party?" Alex asked. He bit into his tortilla and, with eyes closed and his tongue rolling around in his mouth, savored the rolled tortilla slapped with a glob of peanut butter.

"This Saturday," Rudy answered. He put the lid on the peanut butter and started to put it in the cupboard when Estela said, "Leave it out." She got up, blowing on her fingernails. She threw a tortilla on the burner. "Aren't they nice," Estela said, admiring the even strokes on her fingernails. She held them over the burner, drying them even more.

Rudy and Alex smacked their lips and said, "Looks like blood."

"You little jerks," she snapped. "You just don't have any taste."

Rudy and Alex ran out of the house, giggling. They went to the backyard, where Rudy's grandfather sat in the shade of the pomegranate tree. He was whistling while taping a splintered broom.

"See, it's good as new," Grandfather said.

He tapped the broom against his work-hardened palm.

The boys looked at Rudy's grandfather but didn't say anything. They threw themselves on the lawn. Rudy's dog, Chorizo, who was sleeping with his legs straight up in the air, opened his eyes. He had a whiff of their midmorning snack. He rolled over like a barrel and approached the boys, whining for a taste of their tortillas. Each of them tore off a corner, and Chorizo snapped at the sweetness.

"Estela's right," Alex mumbled. "You gotta take something to the party."

"Like what? Tiffany's pretty rich."

"I don't know. Take something she ain't got."

"Like what, Alex?"

Rudy was always bad at choosing gifts. One Christmas he bought his mother a frying pan from a yard sale, and another time he bought his father, also from a yard sale, a fishing pole that snapped when he pulled in a tiny fish.

Gary Soto

Alex looked around the yard. There was a rusty bicycle, lawn chairs, scraggly tomato vines, toys, a rusty push mower, and plastic bags of crushed aluminum cans piled against the garage. Then Alex's eyes fell upon the inner tube hanging awkwardly from the garage roof.

"Like that!" Alex pointed vaguely.

Rudy followed Alex's gaze.

"A garage?" Rudy asked.

"No, the inner tube!"

Rudy raised his head higher and gazed at the inner tube hanging from the roof. His face lit up with excitement. He pictured himself rolling an inner tube to Tiffany's party, and pictured Tiffany's friends all bobbing on the inner tube.

They jumped to their feet, brushing the grass from their pants, and then jumped for the inner tube, which was out of their reach. Even Chorizo, a pretty fat dog, leaped for the inner tube.

Grandfather rose with a sigh from his

chair. "Let me help you, *chamacos*! Give me room."

He poked at the inner tube. He pulled it down with the head of the broom he'd just fixed. Rudy remembered throwing the inner tube up on the roof years before, when he and Estela had come back from a day in the snow. It was the same Christmas he had gotten his mom that frying pan.

"Tiffany doesn't have an inner tube," Alex said. "You'll be *bad*."

"Yeah, I'll be *bad*."

But when they examined the inner tube, they noted an inch-long rip shaped like a clown's mouth. The rip was laughing at them.

"Alex, it's got a rip." Rudy sighed. He poked his finger through the hole. It looked to him as if the clown's mouth was smoking a cigar.

"Don't worry," Grandfather said. He rolled up his sleeves and unbuttoned the top button of his shirt. "I'll fix it in a jiffy.

Give me room!" He took a roll of black electrical tape from his pants pocket.

Rudy and Alex looked at one another. They fell on the lawn, closed their eyes, and listened to the sounds of electrical tape being ripped and taped to the inner tube. They knew that Grandfather would make a mess of it.

"Órale," Grandfather said. "It's all done."

When Rudy and Alex looked up, blinking from the harsh summer light, they were astounded at what they saw. The inner tube was mummified with electrical tape. It looked like something from another planet.

"Did I ever tell you about the time that I worked in a tire shop?" Grandfather said. "Me and Pete Salinas were just out of the army . . ."

Alex and Rudy lay back down, eyes closed. Chorizo joined them, his chest rising and falling and his tail swatting horseflies that had made it into town from the country.

Chapter **4**

"All you gotta do is pound it nine times," Alex explained.

The two boys had left Rudy's grandfather pumping air into the mummified inner tube. They were now searching for another inner tube, one without a rip, one that they could use that summer and later in winter. They were at a gas station, and Alex was revealing one of the last secrets of the civilized world. He said that the soda machine would give up a soda, usually an orange and sometimes an icy root beer, if you banged on the machine nine times.

"Go ahead, try it," Alex said. He poured a handful of Corn Nuts into his mouth. Alex's crunching sounds disturbed three sparrows drinking from a puddle on the ground. They broke skyward toward a tree, bickering.

Rudy looked around to make sure the attendant wasn't watching. He started pounding. *"Uno, dos, tres . . ."*

Alex threw another handful of Corn Nuts into his mouth. When he helped Rudy pound the machine, the gas station attendant, who was sweeping near the air and water hoses, looked up in surprise. His face was smudged with oil, and behind the oil a stubble of beard clung to his face. He leaned the broom against the gas pump and tiptoed toward them in scuffed work boots.

"Seis, siete, ocho . . ." Rudy counted, his smile now ear to ear and bright enough to

light up a room. He stopped before he got to nine and eyed Alex suspiciously. "It better work."

"It works for me," Alex said. He threw a third handful of Corn Nuts into his mouth and licked the salt from his fingers. "Wind up and give it a smack."

Rudy, his smile now a dark line on his determined face, wound up to throw a punch at the belly of the soda machine when the gas station attendant yelled, "Hey, you knuckleheads!"

Rudy jumped. Alex spit out his Corn Nuts.

The attendant grabbed them by the scruff of their necks. "Smart alecks, huh?"

"No, Alex is smarter," Rudy cried, pointing at his best friend. "Huh, Alex?"

"No, you're smarter."

"No, you're smarter. You get better grades."

"That's 'cause my mom helps. You're really smarter."

"No way. You're smarter."

"No, you are."

The gas station attendant had to laugh. "All right, you two. I'll let you go this time. But I'm warning you. *Ándenles, muchachos.* Don't be messin' with the machine."

The boys took off, a few Corn Nuts spilling from Alex's fist. They ran up the street, feeling that they had escaped something terrible. They slowed when they saw a car stalled in the street. Two men had the hood open and were looking inside. One of them yelled, "Hey, *vatos,* why don't you help us."

"Yeah, let's help them push the car," Rudy suggested.

"Yeah, why not," Alex said with excitement.

They hiked up their pants and crossed the street, looking both ways.

"I'll give you a dollar if you can steer this *cochito,*" one of the men said. His cap fit low over his head, just above his eyebrows. "You think you can do it?"

"Sure," said Alex. He had once driven a

tractor, and another time helped steer the car while his father scratched his foot.

"Not you," the man growled. "Him!"

"Me?" said Rudy, pointing a finger at his own chest.

"Yeah, you're smaller. Your friend can help push."

"I guess so," Rudy said. He shrugged his shoulders and hopped into the driver's seat, where he could barely see over the dashboard. The man turned the key in the ignition. He told Rudy that after the car started he should pop the clutch and put the car in first, then press on the accelerator. "Get it up to seven miles first—" The man stopped abruptly to ask, "How old are you?"

"Ten," Rudy answered.

"No, make it ten miles an hour. Can you do that?" the man asked. He took another dollar bill from his pocket. The dollar bill stunk of motor oil.

"Yeah, I think I can."

"*Órale*. Get ready."

The man patted Rudy's knee, closed the

door, and joined Alex and the other man near the trunk. They started pushing their whole weight into the car, which squeaked and moaned. Rudy, wiggling the steering wheel, maneuvered the car, a Mercedes-Benz, he noted, up the street.

"To the right," the man yelled.

Rudy turned the wheel to the right.

"No, to the left," the man yelled.

Rudy turned the wheel to the left.

"No, right, no, left. Keep it straight, little man!"

"Oh, boy," Rudy said. "This is hard. I hope Dad doesn't find out."

When the speedometer registered ten miles an hour, Rudy put the car in gear, released the clutch, and pressed on the accelerator. The car popped, a feather of smoke rising from the tail pipe, and then started moving down the street of its own sweet will.

"It's going," Rudy screamed. "Do something!"

He slid to the passenger seat as the man

with the cap jumped in, revved the engine, and gave Rudy a thumbs-up sign. "Good job." He gave Rudy another oil-stinky dollar. "Do you guys need a ride?"

"Can you take us to a tire shop? We're looking for an inner tube."

"An inner tube?"

"Yeah, I'm invited to a party. I want to take an inner tube."

The man gave Rudy a weird look. "All right, we'll get you there."

They piled into the car. The boys sat in the back. The driver ran a hand over his face. His eyes were small, tired, and tangled with red veins. The veins looked like kindergarten scribbling—messy.

"Hey, Abel," the driver said to the quiet man. "You know a tire shop? There's one on Belmont, *qué no?*"

"Yeah, the one on Belmont, near San Pablo."

They drove in silence. Rudy watched Abel thrust his huge hand in the glove compartment and feel between the cracks of the seats. Abel poked a finger into the ashtray and looked under the floor mats. He lowered the visors. He found two cigarettes and lit one. He crunched the cigarette out after three puffs, and then, with a screwdriver, he started ripping out the radio. The wires sprang up like flowers.

Rudy looked at Alex, who was big-eyed with worry. He wanted to ask, "Do you think this car is stolen?" But he held his tongue and looked out the window. The buildings seemed to go by very fast. His life seemed to go by very fast too. He couldn't wait to be dropped off, alive.

"So what grade you little *cholos* in?" the man with the cap asked. He was steering with both hands on the wheel. His knuckles were tattooed with the word *love.*

"Fourth," Alex volunteered.

"You guys gettin' good grades? You two look pretty smart."

"Yeah," Rudy said, "but Alex is smarter."

"No, you're smarter."

"No, you are."

"No, you remember things better."

"No, you do!"

"Give it a rest," barked the driver. He braked and looked back at the two of them. For a minute, Rudy thought maybe he might wring their necks like chickens.

"You're good kids," he said. "Stay out of trouble."

"We will," Rudy promised. He looked at Alex. "Huh, Alex?"

"Yeah, I promise."

The man gave each of them another oil-stinky dollar and opened the door for them. They climbed out and stepped onto the curb. The Mercedes pulled away with a roar.

"You think that car was stolen?" Rudy asked. In spite of the summer heat, a shiver ran up his back like a zipper. He felt cold, and suddenly full of fear.

"I think so," Alex said. "No, I know so."

A cop car had turned on its lights. It roared after the Mercedes, which pulled away and rounded a corner, tires squealing.

Chapter 5

Rudy and Alex stood in front of Belmont Tire, a one-time gas station and now, as the sign read, Empire of Recapped Tires. A loud air ratchet was bolting a tire onto a car. A tire iron clanged on the ground and a shiny, moon-faced hubcap was popped from a tire and rolled away. A customer's little girl ran after it, squealing and giggling.

"Do you think they'll give us an inner tube?" Rudy screamed over the noise. The tire shop seemed foreign, black with dust. They spied two workers in overalls— neither seemed friendly.

"What?" Alex yelled back.

"I said, do you think they'll give us an inner tube?" Rudy screamed again, this time directly in Alex's ear.

The air ratchet stopped. Quiet filled the air. The little girl returned with the hubcap and gave it to her mother.

"Trust me, they're my personal friends," Alex said, bragging. He hiked up his pants.

"Really? You know them?"

"Really. My uncle worked here. Follow me."

Rudy followed a happily whistling Alex into the yard of the tire shop. Alex kicked a tire out of their way and rolled another one down a passageway like a bowling ball. But they stopped in their tracks when they came upon a dog with mismatched eyes, one blue and one brown. The dog was chained to an air compressor.

"*Cuidado,*" Rudy said. "You didn't say there was a dog!"

"*Ay,*" screamed Alex, jumping back. "Be cool, dog."

The dog yawned at them, yawned and laid its shaggy head on its paws.

"He looks friendly, don't he, Alex?" Rudy asked, his eyes big with fear. Alex had tiptoed behind him, his fingers gripping Rudy's bony shoulders. "Hi, doggie. I have a dog at home. Chorizo. Do you know him?"

"Yeah, do you know Chorizo?" Alex asked. "You'd like him."

There has to be a reason why he's chained, Rudy thought. The *perro* looked dangerous with his two differently colored eyes.

But when the dog yawned a second time and its eyes became watery with sleep, the boys became braver. Alex once again stood tall as he hiked up his pants and muttered to Rudy, "Come on, let's go." They ventured deeper into the yard. Never had they seen so many tires, small ones for motorcycles and really large ones for tractors. Some were even taller than them.

A sloppy pile of inner tubes against the chain-link fence caught their eye. They hurried toward the pile and began to rummage through them.

"Do you think we should ask first?" Rudy asked. He stood up and watched one of the workers. He was on one knee, inflating a tire.

"Nah, this is just junk," he said. "Anyway, they're my personal friends. You know my uncle Lupe?"

"The one with the panther tattoo?"

"Yeah, him. He worked here. They know me."

"Yeah, that's right, they're your 'personal friends.' "

They peeled through inner tubes. Their hands, already dirty from pushing the car, became even dirtier, and the fronts of their shirts became smudged. Mustaches of sweat hung from their upper lips.

"This one is pretty good," Rudy said. He held it around his waist like a Hula Hoop and wiggled his hips like he was dancing.

"Go, brown boy, go!" Alex clapped.

"I'm goin', I'm goin'!" Rudy sang.

Alex was laughing at Rudy's antics when a gloved hand clawed his neck. For a second he thought that the gas station attendant had followed them to the tire shop. He got ready to plead with the hand not to tell his mother. But when he turned, it was one of the men in overalls. His face was lined, and in the lines clung greasy dirt. A front tooth was missing, and in its place a piece of tongue stuck out.

"What're you kids doing?" he growled. A match was stuck in the corner of his mouth.

"Ah, well . . ." Alex stuttered. He looked around to see if there was a way to run without getting caught.

"You're gonna get hurt," the man continued. He spat out the match.

"Ah, well, we need—"

"An inner tube, sir," Rudy interrupted as he stepped in front of Alex. "Just a little one, sir? Please?"

"What for?"

"See, I'm invited to a party. This girl Tiffany invited me. Do you know the Perez family?"

"I know a hundred of 'em. My last name is Perez."

"It is? Are you related to Tiffany?" a surprised Rudy asked.

"No!" the man snapped.

"Well, I guess there are a lot of people named Perez. Her father's a doctor or something. She lives in a nice house."

"Cut to the chase, kid," the man bellowed. "I have work to do. What do you want?"

"An inner tube. I'll even tell her where I got it. Please?"

The man stuck another match, headfirst, in the corner of his mouth. He sized up Rudy and Alex, and then waved. "All right, go ahead. But you get hurt, don't come crying to me."

The man left, and the two of them searched the pile until they found a big inner tube they liked. They left the tire shop with Alex bragging, "See, I told you. They're my personal friends."

At home in the backyard, they pumped air into the inner tube and watched it grow large as a boat. Grandfather, who was weeding the tomato plants, approached the boys, hat tilted and handkerchief tied around his neck. Grandfather whistled and remarked, "That's a heck of an inner tube."

"We got it at Belmont Tire," Rudy said. "From Alex's 'personal friends.' "

"Yeah, they know me there."

"You're takin' it to the party, *qué no*?" Grandfather asked.

"Yeah, this Saturday," Rudy said.

Grandfather ran a hand across his sweaty face. His face became pinched with thought. "That's what we need—a pool."

He turned and gazed dreamily at the yard with its yellow-green lawn. "Yeah, a pool."

Rudy and Alex spent the rest of the afternoon fixing up the inner tube. Alex figured that Rudy could impress Tiffany with a low-riding, *ese* inner tube. They spray-painted the inner tube with splotches of red and yellow and pasted decals and stickers all over it. He let out some air, his fingernails on the stem as the air went *psssssssssss*.

When they finished, Rudy stood back with his hand on his chin, admiring the inner tube. "It's *bad*," he finally announced.

"Yeah, you gonna hit it off with Tiffany." Alex then added, "You oughta ride it in."

"You think so?" Rudy asked, curious to see if he could fit himself into the center. He had ridden in inner tubes when he was young. But now he was older, almost ten, and much heavier. Could he get into the inner tube and hang on? he wondered.

"Give it a try," Alex said. "Just steer

straight. Don't worry if a car hits you, you'll just bounce off."

Rudy, fitted with a helmet and skateboard gloves, groaned as he climbed into the center.

"You ready?" Alex asked.

"Almost," Rudy said. From his pocket he took out a comb that was poking him. "Okay."

Alex pushed and rolled the tube until it began to pick up speed like a train.

"Steer straight," Alex hollered.

"*A la derecha*," Grandfather, now at the side of the house, watering the grass, yelled.

The inner tube bumped and rolled. Rudy screamed, "I hope Mom has insurance for me . . ." as he sped down the street in his low-riding, *ese* inner tube. Rudy rolled and rolled and the food in his stomach—*chicharrónes* and root beer—sloshed about.

Estela was sitting on the fender of a neighbor's car, talking to a friend. The subject was boys.

"Have you dreamed that you lived before?" Estela asked with a faraway smile. Her gold hoop earrings winked with sunlight.

"No," her friend answered.

"Sometimes I get these feelings that I have lived before, and I had all these gorgeous boyfriends. And I—" Estela stopped when she saw an inner tube zip by and Alex running behind it.

"What's that?" her girlfriend asked.

Estela jumped off the fender. "I think it's my stupid brother, Rudy." She propped her hands on her waist and moaned, "I'm gonna have to teach him manners."

The inner tube rolled up the street. It rolled for two blocks before it began to wobble and slow down. Then a teenager who was watching gave it another hard push, and once again Rudy felt like he was in a clothes dryer.

"Go, little dude, go!" the teenager screamed.

"*Ándale*," Alex panted.

The inner tube bounced against a curb and nearly ran into a little girl on her tricycle. Then it headed toward a yard sale. The customers, all bargain seekers, looked up in shock. They dropped their items—clothes, basketballs, lamps, toys—and dashed away as the inner tube rushed toward them.

"Help, Mom," Rudy screamed. "I promise to be good."

The inner tube crashed into the yard sale and Rudy was buried beneath a pile of clothes. Stunned and dizzy, he rose up on his elbows and looked around. A purple hat was on his head, and deep red shame was on his face.

Chapter 6

Rudy returned home dejected, pulling his deflated inner tube. When he had crashed into the yard sale, Alex had hurried away. The inner tube had slammed full force against the sharp edge of the handlebars of a bike. Now it had a foot-long rip. Not even Grandfather's electrical tape could save it.

Rudy's father was leaning over the fender of their Oldsmobile. He was putting in a new set of spark plugs.

"What's up, Little Rudy?" Father asked. He wiped his hands on a greasy rag.

"My inner tube ripped," he answered.

"Ripped!" he said. "After you and Alex decked it out?"

A cloud of sadness swept across Rudy's face. The cloud leaked a tear from the corner of Rudy's eyes.

Father examined the inner tube. He stuck his whole arm into the rip. It was beyond repair.

"Hmmm," he mumbled, hand on his chin. "I got an idea. You come back in five minutes."

Rudy went inside to wash his hands and face and pop a slice of cake into his mouth. When he returned, he was staring at the biggest inner tube in his neighborhood, if not all of Fresno.

"What do you think? Pretty *bad, qué no?*" Father smiled, an air pump in his hands. He was sweaty from pumping, tired, and breathing hard.

"*Papi*, it's great." A happy Rudy beamed. Rudy rolled the huge inner tube around the front yard and, with the neighbor kids watching, bounced on it until he landed on his head. Then his mom called him to dinner.

That night over dinner, the family talked about the party. Mother asked three times, "*Quién es* Tiffany Perez?" and three times Rudy mumbled with his mouth full, "She's just a girl at school. Pass the *papas*."

Estela, though, volunteered more information. "She's a really rich girl. Her brother was in my English class last year."

"Is she a good girl?" Mother asked. She was always concerned about her children's friends.

"Rich?" Father asked, pouring a wide river of chile on his *frijoles*. "I wonder if I ever cut their lawn before. Do you know their address?"

"They live on The Bluffs."

"That's a rich *familia*," Father answered.

Father snapped his fingers. "In fact, I got a mowing job over there. The Ramirez family."

"Mindy Ramirez?" Estela asked. "She's rich too. Her brother's in my math class. He's dumb but cute."

"*Pues*, could be the same family. That house is on *los* Bluffs *también*." Father fumbled through his pockets for a scrap of paper. He held it under the light and read 1356 The Bluffs.

"That's Mindy's address," Estela confirmed. "Her brother is cute!"

"I know Mindy," Rudy said, his mouth full. "She's in my class. I lent her a quarter one time, and she never paid me back."

Grandfather, who was busily eating dinner, said, "That's how the rich get rich. Little quarters add up. Why, back in the fifties, we had . . ."

Grandfather told a story of a young man who arrived from Greece with only a quarter, a quarter that he found in a soda machine on board the ship. According to

Grandfather, the man transformed that quarter into a multimillion-dollar empire.

"I'll have to get my quarter back," Rudy said, sipping his Kool-Aid. "Maybe I can become rich too."

Next morning the family, including an embarrassed Estela, climbed into the Oldsmobile, now transformed, as Father joked, into the Lawnmobile. They had six lawns to cut that day, and Father needed all their help.

"Dad, don't make me do this," Estela begged from the backseat. Estela hid her face in her hands. "I don't want Eric Ramirez, the cutest boy at my school, to see me working. It's too embarrassing!"

"Nobody will say anything," Father said. He shifted the car into reverse and, looking over his shoulder, backed up their large dinosaur of a car. He ran over the curb, jostling the passengers and the equipment in the trunk.

"Work is honorable," Grandfather said after a while. He took a stick of gum and tore it in half. He handed each of his grandchildren a piece. "I've been honorable all my life. *Mira*, look at my hands. *Puro honor!*" His hands were rough as bark, with huge veins riding the surface of his skin.

Estela hid her face even deeper into her hands. She was hating life at that moment.

They did the first two lawns, and then took a break under a tree in Figarden, a rich suburb. Then they cut three more lawns and saved the Ramirez house for last. By then, Estela's face was sweaty. Her knees were grass-stained, her hair tangled from the leaf blower, and her once-polished fingernails were chipped. They looked like broken eggshells to her.

The Oldsmobile rattled up to the Ramirez house, a stately structure that stood tall as a ship.

"Estamos aquí," Father said, and cut the engine. The engine rocked and shuddered, then sighed to a quiet end. They all climbed out. Feeling stiff, Father did a deep-knee bend and stretched his

arms skyward. "Let's start with the front lawn."

"Dad, can I edge this time?" Rudy pleaded. "Come on, Dad."

"Okay, but only if you steer right. I don't want you to mess up."

Grandfather unloaded the mower and edger. Estela took out the brooms and rakes as she moaned to herself. "I can't believe I'm cutting the lawn of one of the most popular boys at school. If Eric sees me I'll die."

Mindy, parting the curtains, looked out the front window. She came out to the front steps and said, "Mom says not to forget the lawn on the side of the house."

"Hi, Mindy," Rudy called.

"Rudy Herrera, is that you?"

"The one and only. I get to edge your lawn. How do you want it?" He pulled the starter on the edger, which coughed blue smoke but didn't start. "You going to Tiffany's party?"

"You mean you're invited?" Mindy asked.

She had a surprised look on her face. Mindy was known to be stuck-up at school. Now Rudy thought she was stuck-up at home too.

"I got an invitation."

Mindy looked at Estela and asked, "Is that your sister?"

Estela pretended to look busy. She lowered her hat over her face.

"Yeah, that's Estela. She's in one of your brother's classes." He turned to Estela and shouted, "Huh, Estela?"

"Rudy, be quiet," Estela snapped. "I'm going to wring your neck when I get home."

Mindy went back inside the house and Rudy pulled the starter on the edger once again. This time, the coughing edger whined into action and the blade spun like the propeller on a helicopter. Rudy lowered his safety goggles and started edging the lawn, orange sparks kicking up against the cement. He edged the front and then the back. He stopped at the pool, next to his grandfather. He shut off the engine and started sweeping.

"Yeah, *es linda*," Grandfather said of the house. He wiped his brow and looked down at Rudy. "You say she owes you a quarter."

"Yeah, plus interest, I guess," Rudy said. Rudy looked up and saw Mindy peeking from behind a curtain. He waved and she ducked out of view.

Grandfather thought a second. Then he asked, "And she's going to the party?"

Grandfather thought even longer. He took off his work gloves and swatted grass from his knees. "Her *hermano* is in Estela's class?"

"That's right."

"Hmmm, well, Little Rudy, I think you should let that quarter pass," Grandfather finally said. "It's too much trouble."

"You're right. You know, after I lent her a quarter, I found a dollar bill at the canal. Me and Alex were looking for frogs. You ever do that, Grandpa?"

"All the time. Back when I was young we had frogs big as baseball mitts."

"*¡De veras!*"

"*Pues sí. Es la verdad.*"

Grandfather smiled and laughed a deep laugh that made his belly jiggle. He bent down and washed his face in the garden hose. Rudy did the same. When he looked up with water dripping from his eyelashes, Mindy was once again looking at him. Rudy waved again and Mindy ducked behind a flowery curtain.

Chapter **7**

An electronic beep sounded when Rudy and Alex entered Everyman's Coin Shop. They closed the door and looked back at their inner tube, which Rudy had chained to a parking meter. Rudy and Alex had debated whether to put money into the meter because, in a way, the inner tube was parked. But they decided to live dangerously and left it chained to the expired meter.

The owner of the coin shop looked up, his eye hideously magnified behind a jeweler's eyepiece, and sized up his two customers. "May I help you gentlemen?" the man asked in a polite voice. His eyepiece dropped into his palm. The owner shook it like dice before he placed it in his shirt pocket.

Rudy and Alex looked around, not sure if the man was talking to them.

"Yes, you two fine customers. How may I be of service?"

Alex nudged Rudy. "Go ahead, ask him."

"Well, sir, is this worth anything? It was made in 1949 in Denver." Rudy uncurled his fist. In his sweaty palm lay the nickel that his father had found while cutting the lawn. Rudy handed the nickel to the man, who brought out his eyepiece and studied the nickel. He hemmed and hawed and ticked the nickel against the glass case. He looked up at the boys. "My dear sirs—" he started to say.

Alex nudged Rudy again. "See! You're going to be rich! Will you buy me a Gameboy?"

"Rich!" Rudy screamed. "I'm going to be rich! Really?"

The two did a quick dance, gave themselves high fives and, gripping the glass case, asked, "How much is it worth?"

The man put his eyepiece back into his shirt pocket. "A nickel," the man concluded.

"Yeah, we know it's a nickel," Rudy said. "But how much?"

"I'm afraid that your nickel is worth a nickel."

Alex closed his eyes in disbelief. "It can't be. It's so old."

"I'm afraid that's the truth."

"No, it can't be," Alex argued again. His face looked desperate. He had talked Rudy into walking two miles to the coin shop because he was sure—dead sure—that the nickel was worth a lot.

The man fumbled through his pockets and brought out a nickel. He looked at the date. "Here, my good friends, is another nickel minted in 1949. You can have it. It's yours."

Rudy took the nickel and peered at it. He gazed intently and concluded, "It is from 1949." Rudy handed it back to the man and turned to Alex. "See, I told you it's not worth anything!"

"How did I know? Remember, you're smarter," Alex said, shrugging his shoulders. "It just seemed so old."

"I'm sorry that I can't help you," the man said, and turned from the boys to answer the telephone.

When they left the coin shop, a policeman was writing up a ticket where they had parked the inner tube.

"*Híjole!*" Rudy screamed. He ran over to the policeman. "Are you giving us a ticket?"

"Is this your inner tube?" the policeman asked. His badge sparkled in the afternoon sun.

"Yeah," Rudy admitted.

The policeman flapped his ticket book

closed. "You can't chain it to a meter. Better move it." The policeman scratched his head and then added, "That's a heck of an inner tube."

"Yeah, I guess so," Rudy said despondently. When the policeman left, Rudy took the 1949 nickel from his pocket and fed the meter. "I may as well put it to use. This car is going to get a ticket if I don't." The meter was ticking down to four minutes.

From the coin shop, Rudy and Alex rolled the inner tube to Francher's Creek, a canal-like river that snaked through south Fresno. "You want to test it for leaks?" Alex asked.

"Probably. Our jeans will dry out quick if they get wet. Anyway, mine could use a wash," Rudy agreed.

They heaved the inner tube into the edge of the creek and got on, Rudy first. Once Alex boarded, they pushed off. They paddled with their hands and with a stick they found floating in the water. They were giddy with excitement. The inner tube floated westward, on a slow but steady current.

"This is fun." Rudy smiled. He cupped his hands and scooped up water. It looked clear and clean, but he hesitated to drink it.

"Yeah, this is *bad*," Alex agreed.

They floated down the creek, their feet dangling in the water. They waved at three small kids on the banks, but their happiness turned sour when the kids started throwing rocks at them. The rocks, though, fell short of their target, and Rudy and Alex just laughed and taunted them.

They floated through a thicket of Johnson weeds, where they picked up a slimy stick. They needed something more to maneuver with, because the water had suddenly become swift. The water cut over some rocks and boards, and lapped the edges of discarded tires.

"Push," Rudy said as he strained to avoid a car fender poking from the water.

"I'm trying," Alex groaned.

They pushed and paddled until the water once again became quiet. They looked down through the doughnut hole of the inner tube. They could see some fish, no bigger than leaves and just as thin. They could see grass waving on the bottom and now and then rocks furred with moss.

"When we grow up, we should join the navy," Alex suggested. He had taken off his T-shirt and draped it over his head, shading him from the hot sun.

"You think so?" Rudy asked. The bike chain dangled like a heavy necklace around his neck. Rudy imagined that it was an anchor, and if they pulled to shore he would tie down the inner tube, just like a boat.

"Yeah. Don't you like water?"

"*Simón*. But you know, I think I like the snow better."

"Really?" Alex thought for a second and then said, "Yeah, it's pretty good until your feet get wet."

"Yeah, one time my toes got so cold, they started bleeding."

"No way."

"*En serio!* I was wearing white socks, and I could tell. Ask my mom."

They floated for an hour, talking about what they would do in the navy, until they got right before a waterfall. Rudy told Alex, "We'd better get out."

They paddled toward the shore just in the nick of time, because the waterfall dropped five feet. At the end of the drop, sharp rocks jutted from the water. With all their strength, they hoisted the inner tube out of the water. They rested on the bank like beached seals. They dozed in the shade, and woke only when the mosquitoes became too furious.

"Let's go," Rudy complained. He poked at his ear, where a mosquito had landed. Blood smeared his fingers, and Alex made a disgusted face when he wiped it on his pants.

They rolled the inner tube along the bank. They became dusty and thirsty, and the mosquitoes wouldn't leave them alone.

They then set the inner tube back into the water and paddled off, two captains of the U.S.S. *Fresno*. They paddled and talked and became so engrossed in their dreams of the navy that they had sailed ten miles out of town.

When they realized how far they had gone, they pulled to the bank and dragged the inner tube from the water. Mosquitoes buzzed at their ears. Their sneakers squished when they walked.

"Alex, I think we're in another town," Rudy said. He smacked a large mosquito from his face.

Alex shaded his eyes with a salute. Everything seemed foreign. He had never seen this town. Alex looked worriedly at Rudy and moaned, "I think we're really in trouble this time."

They sat themselves on the inner tube, two captains on land, and went through their pockets for money. They found two quarters, a stick of wet gum, and a single

Life Saver. They needed those quarters to call Rudy's father, and that Life Saver and stick of gum to sweeten their story of how they had gotten so far from home.

Chapter **8**

The morning sun blazed above the roofs of the neighborhood. And although it was still morning, the little kids from across the street were already running through the sprinklers. Rudy was on the porch bouncing a fluorescent tennis ball against the wall. Father came out, coffee cup in hand. He blew on his coffee and took a sip.

"It's going to be a hot one," he said. His glasses glinted with the sun. His brow was furrowed from squinting at the glare on the street.

"I don't care how hot it gets," Rudy said. He stuffed the ball into his pocket. "I'm going swimming."

Rudy had talked up a storm about the party. He had talked about his inner tube and about Tiffany Perez, the girl in his class. He talked about what he was going to wear and what kinds of dives he would do in the swimming pool. He had told Alex that he was going to try to hold his breath underwater for two minutes.

"Sit down, Little Rudy," Father said. He took a sip of coffee and looked thoughtfully at the sky. "So Tiffany is pretty rich, huh?"

"I think so."

"Well, Rudy, let me give you some advice. You can't eat with your fingers."

"Yeah, I know," Rudy said. "Estela told me already."

"And when you get there, you gotta be polite. You have to make small talk."

"Small talk?"

"Yeah, you got to talk so small that ants can understand what you're saying." He rubbed his chin and thought deeply. "Let me help you. I'll be Mrs. Perez and you be yourself."

"You're going to be Mrs. Perez?"

"*Simón.*"

They stood up, face-to-face. Rudy pretended to knock on the door.

"How's it going, ma'am?" Rudy said as he greeted Mrs. Perez. He had a difficult time seeing Mrs. Perez in the form of his father, especially in a work shirt and thick black glasses.

"No, Rudy. You have to be polite," Father corrected him. "Say, 'Hello, Mrs. Perez. It's a swell day for a swell pool party.' Can you do that? And immediately start making conversation. You could tell her about yourself. Tell her about baseball."

Rudy tried a second time. He knocked and said, "Hello, Mrs. Perez, it's sure a hot day for a hot pool party. I adore fried chicken."

"That's it, *hombre*," Father screamed with delight. He slapped his thighs and said, "Tell her more. *Otra vez*."

"I adore fried chicken *con frijoles*, and *mi perro*, Chorizo, he likes tortillas with peanut butter." Rudy giggled and slapped his own thighs.

"That's it, Rudy," Father encouraged. "Tell her more. Spit it out!"

"I like *huevos con weenies y papas fritas. Me gustan café con leche y helado de coco*." Rudy was smiling from ear to ear as he realized how funny he sounded. He reminded himself of Kid Frost, the rapper from East Los Angeles.

Father slapped his thighs a second time. He took a sip from his coffee cup and smiled broadly at his son. "Rudy, you're gonna be a hit. Bethany-Tiffany-Riffany, or whatever her name is, she's gonna crack up. You know why?"

"No. Why, Dad?"

"You mean you don't know why?"

"No, Dad. Why?"

Father became more serious. "Sit down, Little Rudy." He popped his knuckles and looked around the neighborhood. More children were playing in the sprinklers. The neighbor across the street was washing her car, a Chevy Nova.

"Rudy, we're just ordinary *gente*," Father started. "I work, and El Shorty—your gramps—works. We get by. We're honest. That's it. We get by month to month. That's why she's gonna like you. She's gonna see that you're real. *¿Entiendes?*" He stopped and waved to a neighbor driving past. "Hey, Louie, I got that jack for you. Come by later." The man in the car waved and nodded his head. Father looked at his son with understanding. "Listen, they may be rich folks, but don't worry. Just go and have fun, do some fancy dives in the pool and be nice and . . . bring me home a piece of cake. Okay?"

"Okay, Dad," Rudy said. He understood his father. He understood that while they were everyday workers, they were proud and worked as one—*la familia*. He understood that his father was a good father, serious but not too serious.

Father left with Grandfather to cut lawns. Rudy played with Chorizo and then, struck with a little guilt, he stopped to admire his grandfather's landscaping efforts. His grandfather was working on making a pool in their own backyard. *"Pobre abuelito,"* thought Rudy, "I should help him." Rudy shoveled until he was hot and sweaty and it was time to go to the pool party.

He showered and then, at the foggy bathroom mirror, practiced making polite conversation. "Hello, Mrs. Perez, I adore fried chicken." He raised two splayed fingers and said, "I'll take two pieces." He splashed his father's cologne on his face. "It's a hot day for a swell pool party." He splashed on more cologne. He admired himself in the mirror. "Mrs. Perez," he continued, "I understand that you love turtle soup. I, too, adore turtle soup." He was happy with his small talk, and happy with the way he smelled.

When he came into the kitchen, where Mother was ironing his shirt, he said in a British accent, "Hello, dear mother. I must be off for the pool party."

"Oh, you look so handsome," she said. She pulled at his cheek and said, "*¡Qué bonito!*"

"Mom, I'm ten years old. I'm not a baby."

"You're my baby." She beamed. She had never seen her son so clean, and so dressed up. She sniffed the air. She studied her son with a little smile on her face.

"You smell nice, like your *papi*," she said as she handed him the ironed shirt.

"Well"—he blushed—"I put on a little bit of his cologne."

Mother smiled and asked, "You have a ride?"

"*Simón,*" Rudy said, snapping his fingers. "I got my own wheels, Mom. My inner tube!"

Rudy's ride was his inner tube—taller than his father and wide as Alex. He left the house and rolled it up the street, past the neighbor kids who were once again in the sprinklers. Past his sister who was sitting on a car fender dreaming about boys. Past Louie the neighbor and his dog Charlie. Past other dogs and mothers and the lawns browning under the Fresno sun. A mile north, where the houses turned nice, he passed it all, including his father and El Shorty, whom he didn't see. Their Oldsmobile was stalled. They had run over a board with a nail and now had a flat tire. He didn't hear them scream, "Hey, Little Rudy, we need that inner tube!"

He had on his sunglasses, and his headset on his ears, listening to Kid Frost. Father and El Shorty called and shouted, "Little Rudy, come back!" But Rudy rolled his inner tube toward the pool party, rehearsing inside his head, "Hello, Mrs. Perez, I adore fried chicken."

Chapter **9**

Rudy had rolled his inner tube two miles and now stood in front of a stately house. He took the invitation from his pocket and whispered to himself, "1334 The Bluffs. This must be it." He stuffed the invitation back into his pocket like a Kleenex. "What a big house!" he said. While lugging his inner tube up the steps, it slipped from his fingers. *"Ay,"* he screamed at the inner tube rolling into the street, where it hit and bounced off a Mercedes-Benz. The woman in the car made a face at Rudy. She rolled down her electric window and scolded, "Be careful. This is an expensive car, young man!"

"Sorry," he said. He looked at the car. It seemed unhurt to him. But he added a second time, "Sorry," as the car drove away.

Grunting, he lifted the inner tube and carefully climbed the steps of Tiffany's house. He knocked on the door, then smoothed the front of his shirt. He wondered if his father's cologne was still working.

Tiffany's mother opened the door. She was wearing a fancy dress, and her earrings glittered like the surface of the sea. She greeted him. "Hello, you must be Rudy?"

"That's me, and this is my inner tube," he said happily. He thumped the inner tube with his fist. "My father got it for me when my first one got ripped."

Tiffany's mother gave a shocked look at the huge inner tube. "Why don't you come

in," she started to say, then changed her mind. "Oh, Rudy, why don't you take it around the back. The inner tube is rather large."

"Good idea," Rudy agreed. He didn't want to knock over anything in her house. He started to roll the inner tube away, but then stopped and turned. He remembered his father's advice about small talk. "Mrs. Perez, I understand that you adore turtle soup. What a coincidence. I adore turtle soup too."

The mother looked at Rudy strangely. She closed the front door and Rudy rolled his inner tube to the backyard, which overlooked the bluffs, where a shallow river ran. Now that it was summer, its banks were dry and the water was no bigger than the flow from a garden hose running along a curb.

When Rudy and his inner tube came into view, the kids, who were huddled around the pool or splashing in it, looked up to the shadow of the inner tube. They were curious.

"What's that?" asked one freckle-faced boy with a blown-up duck around his waist.

"Who's that?" a girl snickered. She was hugging a whale and getting ready to dive into the pool.

"Tiffany invited *him* to the party?" another asked.

Mindy was scraping a cracker over a wheel of Brie. She was standing under the arbor and chatting with Eric Contrary Mendoza III. She looked up and moaned, "Oh, it's Rudy Herrera. Look at that thing he's brought!"

While all the kids had fancy pool toys, Rudy proudly rolled in his inner tube. He didn't feel self-conscious. He was, as his father said, *real*. He sized up the pool while he rolled the inner tube toward Tiffany, who was wearing a green T-shirt over a pink swimsuit. She looked beautiful. She looked like her mother, only smaller.

Tiffany smiled at Rudy. "Thanks for coming, Rudy," she greeted him. She looked at the inner tube. She stroked it and stuttered, "Why—why . . . this is the biggest pool toy I've ever seen!"

"Do you like it?" Rudy asked.

"It's smashing," she said.

"Yeah, it's smashing all right," he agreed. "It just smashed into a Mercedes-Benz."

The kids who first thought that the inner tube was weird began to mill around Rudy. They touched and poked at it, curious where Rudy had gotten it and if it was possible for them to get an inner tube too. The red-haired boy slipped the duck pool toy from his waist and asked, "Can we take it into the pool?"

"*Simón*," Rudy said. "That's why I brought it."

Rudy rolled the inner tube to the edge of the pool. He counted as he rocked the inner tube back and forth, "One, two, three . . ." On the count of ten, the inner tube rolled like a huge black shadow into the water and everyone, arms and legs flailing, jumped on it.

Tiffany and Rudy walked to the arbor, where a buffet of colorful food lay. Mindy tagged along reluctantly. "So, how's your summer vacation?" Tiffany asked. She nibbled on a cracker.

"Pretty good. I've been helping my father cut lawns. We even did Mindy's," Rudy said. He bit into a carrot stick and nibbled it like a rabbit. "Right, Mindy?"

Mindy rolled her eyes. "Yeah, you did ours."

"My dad even let me use the edger," Rudy continued.

"Can't you change the subject?" Mindy suggested. She crossed her arms and looked impatient.

Rudy remembered his father's advice—small talk. Rudy grabbed a handful of crackers and offered, "I like turtle soup, but I like *menudo* better. Don't you, Mindy?"

"What?"

"Don't you like *menudo*?" Rudy asked. He tossed a cracker into his mouth. The edge of the cracker poked against the inside of his cheek.

Mindy walked away in a huff. Rudy turned to Tiffany and shrugged his shoulders. "I was just trying to make small talk."

"That's okay," Tiffany said. "She's stuck-up. Come on, let's go swimming." She took Rudy's hand and led him to the pool. They swam and then hopped onto the edge of the inner tube. They were like the bride and groom on a wedding cake.

"It would be *bad* if you and me were in the ocean on an inner tube," Rudy remarked dreamily. "One time I almost drowned, but this inner tube saved me."

"Really?" Tiffany asked.

"Yeah, I was at Avocado Lake with Alex," Rudy dreamed on. "You know Alex, don't you?"

"I think so." Tiffany splashed water on her hot face.

"I got a cramp in my leg, and Alex saved me. Well, actually, it was his dog—Poki. Poki pulled me to shore."

"How exciting!"

Rudy felt good. He was making small talk. "And just a couple of days ago, me and Alex got lost on the inner tube."

"Really?" Tiffany asked. Her eyebrows lifted in interest.

"You ever been to Francher's Creek?"

"No," Tiffany sighed. "My parents usually take us to Hawaii." She splashed water on her thighs.

"Me and Alex were floating on the inner tube there, and we drifted so far we went all the way to Mendota."

"That far?"

"Yeah, and we got in trouble because my dad had to come and get us."

"How exciting! Interesting things seem to happen to you, Rudy."

Rudy felt he was running out of things to say. What could he tell her next? he wondered. Without much thought, he plunged into the water. The inner tube lost its center of balance, and Tiffany toppled over. Underwater, they looked at each other.

They stared and laughed, bubbles large as Ping-Pong balls rising from their open mouths. They rose to the surface laughing. Rudy sneezed because water had gotten up his nose.

"I'm getting out," Tiffany said.

"I'm going to swim for a while," Rudy said. He paddled toward the deep end of the pool. He climbed out of the pool, took a deep breath, and jumped in with a splash. He wanted to see how long he could stay underwater. He counted on his fingers, from left hand to right, back and forth, until he couldn't stand it any longer. He came up, gasping for air. He had stayed under for only fifty-four seconds.

Rudy swam over to a boy who was sitting in a lounge chair, rubbing lotion from a squeeze bottle. Curiously, Rudy watched the boy, then asked, "What are you putting on?"

"A sunscreen, so I don't get dark," he answered. His skin was glistening.

"But you're already dark," Rudy said. He

could see that the boy was Mexican-American. Rudy figured that he was ashamed of the color of his skin, and Rudy was surprised that the boy felt that way.

The boy sat up, shocked. "I beg your pardon!"

Sensing that he had said the wrong thing, Rudy lowered his head into the water and swam to the opposite side of the pool. He got out, toweled off, and joined Tiffany and her mother.

"Tiffany has told me so much about you," her mother said.

"Really? Did she ever tell you I got a home run off Alonso Rodriguez?" Rudy asked. He had started putting food on his plate.

"No, she didn't," her mother said, a twinkle in her eye. She dipped a cookie into a sweet-looking concoction, savoring the taste. "Oh, I love what those caterers do with their ambrosia."

Rudy looked at the food on the table. To him, everything was so small—the small triangles of cheeses, the olives, the sausages, the crackers, and the plates of vegetables. He picked up a tiny cob of corn.

"It's no bigger than my pinkie," Rudy said. "How did they do that?"

"You mean, grow it?" Tiffany asked.

"Yeah. I'm going to tell my mom. She won't believe me."

"I don't know," Tiffany said. "But they're cute, don't you think?"

"Cute?" Rudy wondered. "Yeah, they're kind of cute, all right." He turned the corn cob over in his hands and was going to put it in his mouth like a cigar, letting it dangle from his lips. But he knew better. Instead, he nibbled it and remarked, "It's a swell day for a swell pool party."

Tiffany's mother was called away. Rudy and Tiffany went to the gazebo, where a harpist was playing. He had never been up close to a harp, and now he was tapping his bare foot to the music. When she finished playing, he put down his plate of food and

applauded. He asked, "Do you know 'Louie Louie'?"

The harpist shook her head.

"Do you know '96 Tears'?"

Again the harpist shook her head.

"How 'bout 'Woolly-Bully'?"

When the harpist shook her head a third time, Rudy whispered to Tiffany, "I guess she must be a beginner."

Rudy swam all afternoon and was one of the last to leave the party. His eyes were red from the chlorine. His inner tube was almost flat because everyone had used it.

"Thanks for coming," Tiffany said. Her eyes sparkled like sunlight on water.

"Thanks for inviting me. That was fun," Rudy said. To Tiffany's mother, he said, "You have a nice house, Mrs. Perez."

He left and dragged his inner tube home, happy that the summer sun was riding on his back.

Chapter 10

Rudy arrived home tired from the two-mile walk. He tossed his inner tube in the garage, and before going inside, he looked at the kidney-shaped hole Grandfather had dug for his swimming pool. Rudy was amazed at how far down Grandfather had dug. Rudy knew that he had worked hard because the dirt was hard as his fist and just as brown.

"It's *bad*," Rudy said. "I'll invite Tiffany

over when we get it done." Rudy felt a happiness blossom inside himself. He was proud of his family, and proud of his grandfather.

Rudy went inside, his towel over his shoulder. The smell of baking enchiladas filled the kitchen.

"*¿Cómo fué la fiesta?*" Mother said. She was at the kitchen counter, dicing a red onion. Her eyes stung from its vapors.

"It was fun, Mom," Rudy said. "Tiffany's pretty nice."

"Is she going to invite you again?"

"*Quizás*. Probably if she has another pool party."

Rudy went to his bedroom, changed into his everyday clothes, and went outside to play slap ball against the side of the garage. When he heard their Oldsmobile, he turned and waved. Father and Grandfather were home from work.

"Hey, Little Rudy," his father said. He looked tired and hot. His knees were streaked with grass stains.

Grandfather got out of the car. His pockets bulged with electrical tape. He was wearing a Giants baseball cap.

"Where did you get that cap!" Rudy asked.

"The best of the best—Juan Marichal," Grandfather answered. He took it off and put it on Rudy's head, backward.

"And hey, didn't you see us?" Father asked. He sat on the back porch and unlaced his work boots.

"See you?" Rudy asked with a confused look on his face.

"Yeah, me and Gramps got a flat. Did you have *tus ojos cerrados?*" He turned his boot over and sand rained onto the ground.

"I didn't see you, Dad." Rudy was more than confused. He was embarrassed that he hadn't seen his father.

"We couldn't miss you. That inner tube was as big as Godzilla."

Father went inside to wash up and Grandfather went to the backyard. He took up a shovel and Rudy grabbed another one.

They began to dig, each of them with the dream of a swimming pool glistening under the Fresno sun.

"*La comida*," Mother called from the kitchen window.

They stuck their shovels in the dirt and went inside to wash up.

While Rudy was in the bathroom, he splashed cologne on his face and arms. He looked in the mirror. "Hello, Mrs. Perez, it's a swell day for a swell pool party. I adore fried chicken." He held up two splayed fingers. "I'll take two pieces." He splashed his face with more cologne and then skipped to the dinner table.

But Grandfather was too tired to eat at the table. He rolled up a tortilla, dipped it into salsa, and took it to his recliner.

The rest of the family sat down to eat.

"So how was the party?" Father asked. He smothered his enchiladas with chile.

"It was okay," Rudy said. He shoved a forkful of *fideo* into his mouth. "Tiffany has a pretty nice house."

"They're pretty rich, *qué no?*"

Rudy scooped up a puddle of *frijoles*. "Yeah, they're rich."

Estela asked, "What kind of food did you eat?"

Rudy wiped his mouth and said, "You wouldn't believe it, but they had food small as my pinkie."

"That small, huh?" Father asked.

"Yeah, I ate three corns, and I didn't get filled up." Rudy raised his glass of purple Kool-Aid. When he drank, his Adam's apple went up and down like an elevator. He looked at his father's dark arm. "Dad, you need a sunscreen?"

"A sunscreen!" His father looked down at his arm thick with muscle. "*Puro Mexicano*. That's me."

"I know. But I saw a boy use sunscreen at the party."

"I'm naturally dark. I'm almost all Aztec."

"Really?" Rudy asked. He liked the idea of being Indian.

"*Simón, ese!*"

Rudy laughed at his father and looked at his mother. "Mom, is Dad really Aztec?"

She gave her husband a look of *mentiroso* but said, "*Claro.*"

Rudy then said, "Mom, your food is better." He cut an enchilada, which sent up a curl of steam, and let roll in his most Mexican voice, "*Qué rrrrrrico.*"

"*Ay, mi santito,*" Mother said. "You want some more?"

Rudy nodded his head and his mother brought a pan of enchiladas, warm from the oven.

While the Herrera family ate, Grandfather—El Shorty—dozed in the living room. The book *How to Build a Swimming Pool* lay on his lap. He was snoring loudly, so loudly that Rudy said, "Gosh, Grandpa is cutting some good zzzzzs." It was the truth. His dreams were wide and deep—as clear and sparkling as any pool in the sun.